UNICORNS
ARE THE
WORST!

ISBN 978-1-338-80660-1

12 11 10 9 8 7 6 5 4 3 2 1   21 22 23 24 25 26

Printed in the U.S.A.   40

First Scholastic printing, October 2021

Book design by Chloë Foglia and Alex Willan
The text for this book was set in Rockwell.
The illustrations for this book were rendered digitally.

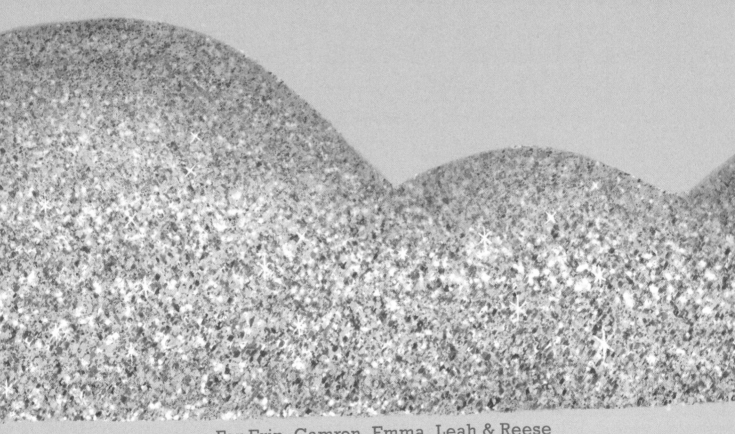

For Erin, Camron, Emma, Leah & Reese

UNICORNS ARE THE WORST!

By ALEX WILLAN

SCHOLASTIC INC.

For hundreds of years I have gone about completing my important goblin business in peace.

From documenting spells,

to gathering ingredients for spells,

Unicorns R the BEST!

Unicorns ARE **MAGICAL**

#1

BLAH·BLAH·BLAH

That's true, but a lot of things are magical. Like elves and . . .
fairies and . . .
what's the other one . . .
elves, fairies, aaaaannnnd . . .
oh, right . . .
The Big Book of Magical Creatures
Dragons: A Survival Guide
Elvish Folklore
Fabulous Fairies

GOBLINS

I have studied the forgotten magic
that lies deep within the earth.

fig.1

fig.2

I know spells that can transform socks into slugs,

fig.3

fig.4 *

I can turn broccoli into ice cream,

*Still tastes like broccoli.

a

b

c

fig.5

and I have mastered the three-strand braid!

But despite all of this, does anyone ever ask to have a Goblin-themed birthday party?

PARTY

$19.99 $7.99 $15.99

TUB O' GLITTER

UNICORN RING TOSS

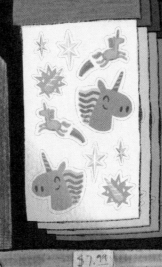

$12.99 $17.99 $7.99 $3.99

N THE HORN

ON THE

ICORN

$29.99

SLUG CHOW

And the glitter . . .

SO.

MUCH.

GLITTER!

Do you realize how hard it is
to get glitter out of a smock?

They are constantly playing their instruments.
News flash, unicorns: Not everyone likes harp music!

And the tea parties!

so. MANY.
TEA PARTIES!

a unicorn's horn is more than just pointy.

ALEX WILLAN

grew up in Louisville, Kentucky, where he was seldom seen without his sketchbook in hand. Alex has exhibited in art galleries and has painted murals, theater sets, and squirmy kids' faces, but his true love has always been children's books. Alex is also the author and illustrator of *Jasper & Ollie* and *Jasper & Ollie Build a Fort*. He lives in Chicago with his dog, Harley.